Hush, Little Baby

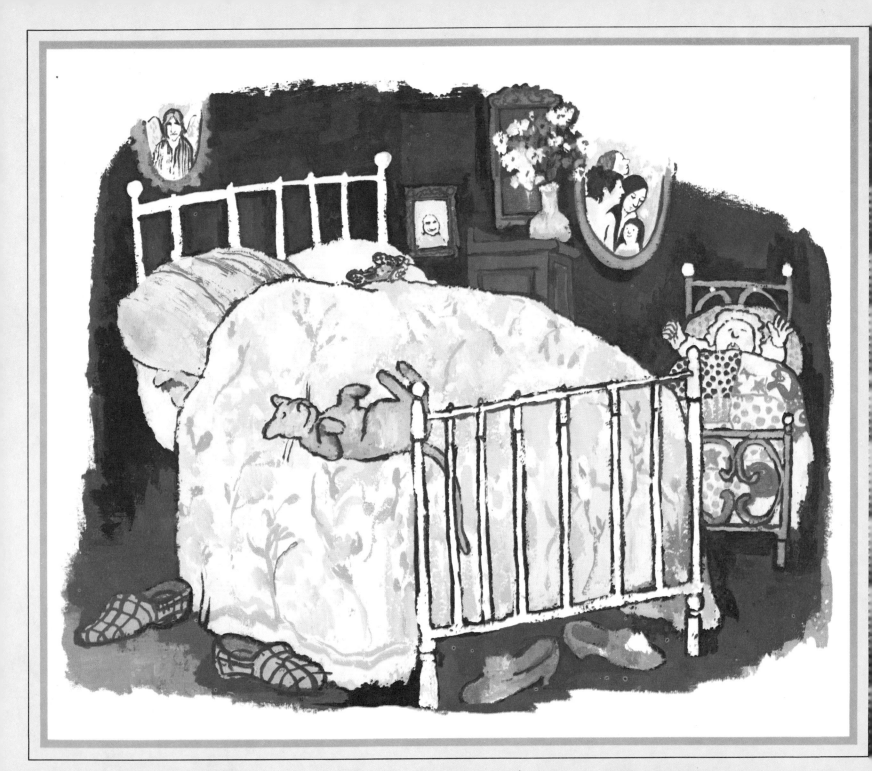

MARGOT ZEMACH

Hush, Little Baby

E. P. Dutton & Co., Inc.   New York

Library of Congress Cataloging in Publication Data

Main entry under title: Hush, little baby

SUMMARY: A baby is promised a strange assortment
of things, from a mockingbird to a horse and cart—
all for not crying.

[1. Lullabies.   2. Folk songs]   I. Zemach, Margot.
II. Title.
PZ8.3.H952   [E]   76-5477   ISBN 0-525-32510-7

Published simultaneously in Canada by Clarke,
Irwin & Company Limited, Toronto and Vancouver

Book design and title hand-lettering by Riki Levinson
Printed in the U.S.A.   First Edition
10 9 8 7 6 5 4 3 2 1

780/30

For Auntie Rees of Crooms Hill Grove, London,
with our love

Hush, little baby,
Don't say a word,

Poppa's gonna buy you
a mockingbird.
If that mockingbird won't sing,

Poppa's gonna buy you
a diamond ring.
If that diamond ring turns brass,

Poppa's gonna buy you
a looking glass.
If that looking glass gets broke,

Poppa's gonna buy you
a billy goat.
If that billy goat won't pull,

Poppa's gonna buy you
  a cart and bull.
If that cart and bull turn over,

Poppa's gonna buy you
a dog named Rover.

If that dog named Rover won't bark,

Poppa's gonna buy you
a horse and cart.

If that horse and cart

fall down,

You'll still be the sweetest
baby in town.

Hush, Little Baby

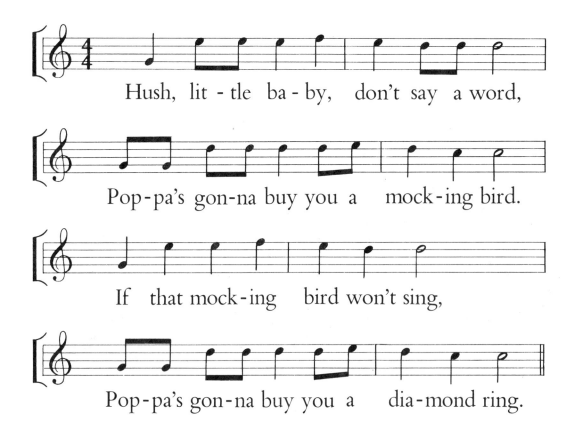

Hush, lit - tle ba - by, don't say a word,

Pop-pa's gon-na buy you a mock-ing bird.

If that mock-ing bird won't sing,

Pop-pa's gon-na buy you a dia-mond ring.

If that diamond ring turns brass,
Poppa's gonna buy you a looking glass.
If that looking glass gets broke,
Poppa's gonna buy you a billy goat.

If that billy goat won't pull,
Poppa's gonna buy you a cart and bull.
If that cart and bull turn over,
Poppa's gonna buy you a dog named Rover.

If that dog named Rover won't bark,
Poppa's gonna buy you a horse and cart.
If that horse and cart fall down,
You'll still be the sweetest baby in town.

MARGOT ZEMACH is the distinguished illustrator of many books, including *Mommy, Buy Me a China Doll, The Judge,* and *Duffy and the Devil,* winner of the Caldecott Medal (all published by Farrar, Straus and Giroux).

She says that she began to consider *Hush, Little Baby* a "tried and true" lullaby after singing it to her daughter Rebecca every night for a year and a half. During that time, the pictures of a large, untidy Mum, downtrodden, anxious Dad, and squalling baby seemed to form themselves in her mind—undoubtedly with a British flavor due to the fact that she was then living in London.

The artist and her four daughters now live in Berkeley, California.

The title is hand-lettering and the other display and text type was set in Griffo Alphatype. The full-color illustrations were painted with tempera. The book was printed by offset at A. Hoen & Co.